Dear Parents:

Congratulations! Your child is taking the first steps on an exciting journey. The destination? Independent reading!

STEP INTO READING® will help your child get there. The program offers five steps to reading success. Each step includes fun stories and colorful art or photographs. In addition to original fiction and books with favorite characters, there are Step into Reading Non-Fiction Readers, Phonics Readers and Boxed Sets, Sticker Readers, and Comic Readers—a complete literacy program with something to interest every child.

Learning to Read, Step by Step!

Ready to Read   Preschool–Kindergarten
• big type and easy words • rhyme and rhythm • picture clues
For children who know the alphabet and are eager to begin reading.

Reading with Help   Preschool–Grade 1
• basic vocabulary • short sentences • simple stories
For children who recognize familiar words and sound out new words with help.

Reading on Your Own   Grades 1–3
• engaging characters • easy-to-follow plots • popular topics
For children who are ready to read on their own.

Reading Paragraphs   Grades 2–3
• challenging vocabulary • short paragraphs • exciting stories
For newly independent readers who read simple sentences with confidence.

Ready for Chapters   Grades 2–4
• chapters • longer paragraphs • full-color art
For children who want to take the plunge into chapter books but still like colorful pictures.

STEP INTO READING® is designed to give every child a successful reading experience. The grade levels are only guides; children will progress through the steps at their own speed, developing confidence in their reading.

Remember, a lifetime love of reading starts with a single step!

Visit us on the Web!
StepIntoReading.com
randomhousekids.com

Educators and librarians, for a variety of teaching tools, visit us at RHTeachersLibrarians.com

ISBN 978-0-7364-3536-9 (trade)—ISBN 978-0-7364-3537-6 (ebook)
ISBN 978-0-7364-8238-7 (lib. bdg.)

Printed in the United States of America
10 9 8 7 6 5 4 3 2

STEP INTO READING®

2

STEP

READING WITH HELP

DISNEY · PIXAR

INSIDE OUT

MOM, DAD, AND ME

by Christy Webster

Random House 🏠 New York

This is Riley.
She lives with
her mom and dad
in a small town.

Mom and Dad take
good care of Riley.
They all love each
other very much.

Mom is smart and kind.
She gives the best hugs!

Dad is silly and fun.

He likes to play games.

Mom, Dad, and Riley
love their home.
There is a lake
near their house.

It is the perfect place
for Riley to grow up!

Riley, Mom, and Dad
love to play hockey.

Hooray!

Riley scores a goal!

Riley has made
lots of memories
over the years.
Some are happy.

Some are sad.

Some are both!

One day,
Dad gets a new job
in a big city.

They sell their house
and move away.

Moving is hard
for Riley.
It is sad to leave
her old life behind.

The new house
is nothing
like the old one.
It does not feel
like home.

Riley goes
to a new school.
Will she make
new friends?

Mom has an idea.

She helps Riley join

a new hockey team!

Riley likes being
part of the team.
After a while,
she makes lots
of new friends.

Mom and Dad are

still her biggest fans.

Riley learns that
some things change.

But Mom and Dad will
always be there for her.

Family is forever.